THE THREE MUSKETEERS

Dorling **DK** Kindersley

LONDON, NEW YORK, SYDNEY, DELHI, PARIS,
MUNICH and JOHANNESBURG

A RETELLING FOR YOUNG READERS
BASED ON AN ORIGINAL NOVEL BY DUMAS

Project Editor Rebecca Smith
Designer Tanya Tween
Senior Editor Alastair Dougall
Production Steve Lang
Managing Art Editor Jacquie Gulliver
Picture Research Frances Vargo
DTP Designer Kim Browne and Jill Bunyan

First American Edition, 2000
2 4 6 8 10 9 7 5 3 1
First published in the United States by
Dorling Kindersley Publishing, Inc.
95 Madison Avenue
New York, NY 10016

Leitch, Michael.
The three musketeers / by Alexandre Dumas ; retold by Michael
Leitch. – – 1st American ed.
p. cm. – – (Dorling Kindersley Classics)
Summary: In seventeenth-century France, young D'Artagnan initially
quarrels with, then befriends, three musketeers and joins them in
trying to outwit the enemies of the king and queen. Illustrated
notes throughout the text explain the historical background of the story.
ISBN 0-7894-5456-4
1. France – –History– –Louis XIII, 1610–1643 Juvenile fiction.
[1. France– –History– –Louis XIII, 1610–1643 Fiction. 2. Adventure
and adventurers Fiction.] I. Dumas, Alexandre, 1802–1870. Trois
mousquetaires. English. II. Title. III. Series.
PZ7.L53717Th 2000
[Fic] – –dc21
99–39929
CIP

see our complete
catalog at
www.dk.com

Color reproduction by Bright
Arts in Hong Kong
Printed by Dai Nippon in China

10/00
BH

DORLING KINDERSLEY CLASSICS

THE THREE MUSKETEERS

ALEXANDRE DUMAS

Retold by MICHAEL LEITCH

Illustrated by
VICTOR AMBRUS

DK

A Dorling Kindersley Book

D'Artagnan, the
dashing young hero

CONTENTS

Richelieu, the powerful
and ruthless Cardinal

Milady, the
scheming spy

Porthos, the
extravagant musketeer

Aramis, the secretive musketeer

Athos, the
melancholy musketeer

*Rochefort, the mysterious
man from Meung*

*Queen Anne, the beautiful
wife of King Louis*

*Monsieur Bonacieux,
a cowardly landlord*

*Madame Bonacieux,
the Queen's linen maid*

*Louis XIII, the
King of France*

*Duke of Buckingham,
the romantic Englishman*

INTRODUCTION

Swords, duels, intrigues, romance – over 150 years after it was written, *The Three Musketeers* continues to delight all who read it. The hero of the story is d'Artagnan, based on a real French musketeer. He is an ambitious young man who is determined to prove himself in the highest circles and become a musketeer. Fascinated by the glamor and danger of a musketeer's life during the time of King Louis XIII, the 19th-century novelist Alexandre Dumas transforms the historical characters and politics of the early 17th century into a legendary story.

Dumas's ability to make history come alive is extraordinary. As we travel with d'Artagnan from his provincial home in southern France to the sophistications of Parisian life, Dumas shows us the dangerous world of court politics. Plots, rivalries, spies, and informers lurk everywhere, and as d'Artagnan soon discovers, there are many who do not want him to survive.

But help is at hand. Three musketeers – Athos, Porthos, and Aramis – are all fighting for their country, their queen, and most importantly, for each other. Together they take on the might of Cardinal Richelieu, the scheming spy Milady, and the rebellious people of La Rochelle with a spirit of adventure that seems inexhaustible.

With color photographs and paintings to show life as it was lived in the days of the musketeers, this Dorling Kindersley Classic captures the spirit of Dumas's story. Duels are fought, identities hidden, murders committed, lives threatened, and all this as the musketeers battle to prove that they are the real heroes of their time.

17th-century Paris: city of intrigue

D'ARTAGNAN'S FRANCE

The story of *The Three Musketeers* begins in France in 1625 – a time of great political and religious turmoil. The Catholic king, Louis XIII, and his adviser, Cardinal Richelieu, are determined to keep the French Protestants (known as Huguenots) in check. They are also seeking to further France's European interests against Spain. Hideous murders and drawn-out civil wars have been plaguing the country for many years. Into the very center of this world of divided loyalties and dangerous alliances comes d'Artagnan, our young, hot-headed hero, determined to become a king's musketeer.

Increasing hostility between Protestants and Catholics in France during the 16th century led to the horrors of St. Bartholomew's Eve in 1572. In one night, over 2,000 Protestants were slaughtered.

THE CHARACTERS

The characters in The Three Musketeers *are all based on historical figures from the 17th century. Although the author, Dumas, does invent some of the events, much of the story really did happen.*

D'Artagnan
The hero of *The Three Musketeers*, d'Artagnan, was indeed a great musketeer, who came from a prosperous family in Gascony. The real d'Artagnan served Louis XIV, not Louis XIII and went to Paris in 1640 (15 years later than the story claims). He became captain-lieutenant of the King's Musketeers and was killed in action in 1673.

Louis XIII
Son of Marie de Medici and Henry IV, Louis (1601–43) was only nine when he was crowned king. By 15, he had married Anne of Austria and had assumed full control of his court duties. Secretive, pious, sometimes ruthless and cruel, Louis was a more skillful politician than Dumas gives him credit for.

Cardinal Richelieu
Armand-Jean du Plessis (1585–1642), later known as Richelieu, was made Cardinal in 1622. After the king, he was the most powerful man in France. Richelieu was an intelligent operator who maintained his position in the Church and the State despite frequent plots against him.

Queen Anne
Anne of Austria (1601–66) was the daughter of King Philip III of Spain. She was only 14 when she became the wife of Louis XIII, and they were never close.

Duke of Buckingham
George Villiers (1592–1628) was a favorite of the English monarchy and gained great wealth, but his arrogance and Catholic sympathies made him widely disliked.

These are dangerous times for the guardian of the Queen's diamonds.

London

Dover

Calais

Portsmouth

Boulogne

Armentières

Lille

Béthune

Near the Belgian border, the musketeers take the law into their own hands.

Amiens

D'Artagnan finds that convents are not as safe as they seem.

Beauvais

The most deadly of the cardinal's spies travels in style.

Chantilly

Paris

PARIS

Most of the action in The Three Musketeers takes place in Paris. The king, cardinal, musketeers, and Milady all live near one another in the great city.

The musketeers' favorite wine comes from the Anjou region.

The cardinal has set up camp near La Rochelle.

La Rochelle

Tension is building in La Rochelle, a Huguenot stronghold.

Meung

River Seine

D'Artagnan comes from Gascony, a region in the southwest of France.

Tarbes

THE LIFE OF A MUSKETEER

The king's musketeers were the most glamorous company in the French army. There were only about a hundred musketeers, and most of them were of aristocratic birth. Only men who had proved themselves in the heat of battle were admitted. The musketeers' main duty in peace time was to act as the king's escort; otherwise they could do much as they liked. The three musketeers of Dumas's story – Athos, Porthos, and Aramis – all really existed, although the author invented much of their history and character.

En garde!
The King's Musketeers prided themselves on their peerless swordfighting skills. As Dumas records, they frequently clashed in duels with a rival elite company, the guards of Cardinal Richelieu.

Swashbuckling – the musketeers and Richelieu's guards clash in The Three Musketeers (1973).

Civilians join the army – a 17th-century print by Jacques Callot.

Volunteers only
In those days, most sons of the nobility either went into the Church or volunteered to join the army. Pay was low, and soldiers had to buy their own equipment, which could be extremely expensive. To line their pockets, ordinary soldiers and officers relied on winning plunder from the enemy.

Pike

Matchlock mechanism

Priming pan and cover

Rope slow-match

Trigger

Trigger guard

Wooden rest to support musket when firing

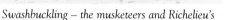

Matchlock musket
The matchlock mechanism used a lighted fuse to ignite powder in the priming pan. This in turn ignited the charge in the barrel, firing the ball.

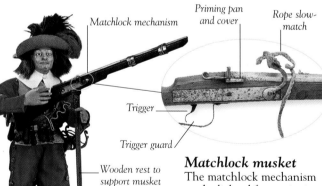

Gunpowder belt
Ammunition was kept on a belt called a bandoleer, which slipped over the arm and head. Each of the 12 flasks held a charge of gunpowder. Musket balls were kept in a little bag.

Top guns
The musketeers took their name from a new type of gun, called a musket.

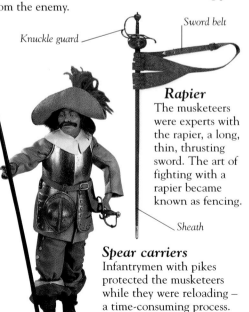

Knuckle guard

Sword belt

Rapier
The musketeers were experts with the rapier, a long, thin, thrusting sword. The art of fighting with a rapier became known as fencing.

Sheath

Spear carriers
Infantrymen with pikes protected the musketeers while they were reloading – a time-consuming process.

Anything goes

With few military duties, the musketeers had plenty of time for love affairs. Dumas portrays them as men of honor, ready to fight a duel at a moment's notice to protect their own reputation, or a woman's. However, they also have a heartless side and relish romantic intrigues. For d'Artagnan and the three musketeers, all is fair in love.

Flirting – Barbara La Marr and Douglas Fairbanks in the 1921 film of The Three Musketeers.

Jolly good fellows – Van Heflin, Gene Kelly, Gig Young, and Robert Coote in The Three Musketeers *(1948).*

Team spirit

As a small, select band of young men, the King's Musketeers were fiercely loyal to each other. This spirit is perfectly summed up by their famous cry, "All for one and one for all!"

THE REAL MUSKETEERS

The three musketeers in Dumas's story came from Gascony, as did d'Artagnan. Since little was known about their lives and personalities, Dumas was free to invent as he liked.

Athos

Athos's real name was Armand de Sillégue, and he was the squire of Athos, a small village in Gascony. Monsieur de Tréville, captain of the musketeers, was a distant relative, which may have helped Athos to become a musketeer. He died in Paris in 1643, probably in a duel. Dumas portrays Athos as a deep thinker and a natural leader, with a mysterious, tragic past.

Porthos

Porthos's real name was Isaac de Portau. In reality, he was not yet a musketeer when d'Artagnan arrived in Paris in 1640, but joined three years later. Dumas gives him a boisterous, good-humored, pleasure-loving personality. He loves fancy clothes, good food, wine, women, and song.

Aramis

Aramis was Henry d'Aramitz, a squire and landlord of Aramitz, in Gascony. Like Athos, he was related to de Tréville; he joined the musketeers in 1640. Dumas describes him as amiable and extremely handsome, but also rather devious. He is particularly adept at conducting secretive romances, while claiming to be studying to enter the Church.

La Rochelle

The siege of La Rochelle, in northern France, was one occasion when the musketeers were involved in serious action and helped to relieve a fortress. The port was a stronghold of Protestant Huguenot rebels. The French army, commanded by Richelieu, starved the townsfolk into submission by building an earthwork across the harbor, preventing the English navy from bringing in supplies and reinforcements.

Cardinal Richelieu at the siege of La Rochelle.

Chapter one

THE THREE GIFTS

ON THE FIRST MONDAY of April 1625 a young man arrived outside the Jolly Miller inn in the market town of Meung. He was riding an old horse of a peculiar yellow color, whose awkward, plodding walk made passers-by smile. However, they hid their mirth when they saw the rider's stern expression.

The young man dismounted. His name was d'Artagnan. He was eighteen years old, tall, with proud, fierce eyes and a jutting jaw. The sword he wore was so long it nearly reached his ankles. He had set off for Paris from his parents' home in Gascony, taking with him three gifts from his father – a purse of 15 crowns, the yellow nag, and a letter of introduction to Monsieur de Tréville, Captain of the King's Musketeers.

An elegantly dressed, dark-haired man with a scar on his cheek was standing in one of the inn's ground-floor windows. He was talking with two men, who burst into fits of laughter. D'Artagnan, sure they were making fun of him, eyed him fiercely. "Hello, there! Yes, you, sir," he cried. "Tell me what you are laughing at!"

"That horse is a buttercup," the man coolly replied, "or has been. Its color is common in flowers, yet very rare in horses."

Scarlet with rage, d'Artagnan drew his sword and charged at the man, who had to leap back to save his life. The stranger's friends, helped by the innkeeper, rushed out and fell on d'Artagnan with sticks and shovels. He fought hard, but at last a fierce blow on the forehead knocked him senseless.

When he came to, he was lying on a bed upstairs. The innkeeper, anxious to be rid of this troublesome guest, helped him down to the kitchen. Through the open door, d'Artagnan glimpsed the stranger standing by a carriage. Framed prettily in the carriage window was the head of a young woman with fair hair, large blue eyes, and rosy lips.

"So, his Eminence orders me to ..." she was saying.

"To return at once to England, and warn him the moment the Duke leaves London, Milady," the stranger confirmed.

D'Artagnan staggered out into the yard. "This time you won't escape me!" he cried.

But the stranger leaped onto his horse, and he and the lady sped away in opposite directions.

Gascony
D'Artagnan is from Gascony, in southwest France. Gascons had a reputation for being courageous, ambitious and hot-tempered, and many became fearless soldiers. Brought up in the country, d'Artagnan is an innocent in the wicked ways of the world.

The woman had fair hair and large blue eyes.

Traveler's rest
In the days when people traveled on horseback or in coaches, they broke their long journeys at roadside inns. There they could spend the night, have a meal, and either rest their horses or obtain fresh ones. Inns were places where all classes of society rubbed shoulders.

"Coward!" d'Artagnan shouted. Then, weak from his injuries, he collapsed in the road. "But how beautiful she is," he murmured.

"Who? Who is?" asked the innkeeper, coming up.

"My lady," mumbled d'Artagnan. And for the second time that day he passed out.

Chapter two

MONSIEUR DE TRÉVILLE

A DAY LATER d'Artagnan was well enough to resume his journey. He reached into his pocket to pay his bill. His purse was still there – but his letter of introduction to Monsieur de Tréville had disappeared! He turned angrily on the innkeeper, who nervously answered, "It must have been stolen."

"Stolen? By whom?"

"By the gentleman with the scar, sir. He went through your pockets after you were knocked out."

Vowing to report the theft to the king himself, d'Artagnan set off for Paris. When he reached the city, he sold his yellow horse and took a room.

The following morning he went to meet Monsieur de Tréville who, according to his father, was the third most important man in France after the king and the king's closest adviser, Cardinal Richelieu.

As d'Artagnan entered the study of the great man, de Tréville called out irritably, "Athos! Porthos! Aramis!"

Two musketeers, Porthos and Aramis, entered. They blushed in shame while their chief scolded them for fighting the previous evening with their old enemies, the cardinal's guards.

De Tréville scolded Porthos and Aramis for fighting.

From a window, d'Artagnan glimpsed the mysterious man.

To be a musketeer
The musketeers were the king's bodyguards and had a stylish, dashing image. No wonder young d'Artagnan wants to join them. Their commander, Monsieur de Tréville (1598–1672), really existed. Like d'Artagnan, he came from Gascony, and he rose to become captain-lieutenant of the musketeers.

In the struggle Athos had been wounded.

Satisfied with their apologies, Monsieur de Tréville dismissed them and turned to d'Artagnan.

"And what can I do for you?" He frowned.

"Sir, I wish to become a musketeer, though I fear I am asking too great a favor."

D'Artagnan told him about the stolen letter of introduction from his father, and the mysterious man from Meung's meeting with the beautiful lady. De Tréville stared hard at him. "Is this country boy as honest as he seems?" he wondered.

"Or could he be a spy in the pay of the cardinal?"

De Tréville decided to give the hotheaded young man a chance. He picked up a pen and wrote a letter of recommendation to the director of the Royal Academy, where d'Artagnan could learn horsemanship, fencing, and courtly manners. He was just about to give it to d'Artagnan when the young man, who had been gazing dreamily out of the window, suddenly turned red with anger and dashed out of the room crying, "Ha! He won't get away this time!"

"Who on earth do you mean?" demanded Monsieur de Tréville, leaping from his chair.

"The thief!" exclaimed d'Artagnan. "The traitor!"

And he disappeared.

The Carmelite nuns
Renowned for their austerity, the Carmelite nuns wore no shoes, took vows of silence, and cut themselves off from the world. Their convent stood near the center of Paris, and the quiet meadow nearby was a popular place for duels. The convent, which had no windows, has been demolished, but the nearby church (pictured above) still stands.

The handkerchief
A handkerchief, perhaps dipped in perfume and bearing its owner's distinctive insignia, was a token of a lady's love. Aramis is furious with d'Artagnan for accidentally revealing that he is having a secret love affair with a well-known lady.

Chapter three

MUSKETEERS AND GUARDS

D'ARTAGNAN CHARGED head first down the stairs and ran straight into a musketeer, who howled in pain. "I'm sorry," said d'Artagnan, "but I'm in a great hurry."

"You think that's enough of an apology?" cried the musketeer, his face pale as death, for this was the very Athos who had been wounded the previous evening.

"I said I'm sorry, and that is quite sufficient, I think," replied d'Artagnan, holding his head high.

"You are by no means polite," returned Athos. "We will duel at midday near the Carmelite convent. And don't be late."

"Very well," cried d'Artagnan, and he rushed off in pursuit of the mysterious stranger. Seconds later a gust of wind blew something across his path – he was trapped in Porthos's voluminous cloak.

D'Artagnan ran straight into a musketeer, who howled in pain.

"Great heavens!" shouted Porthos. "Do you always shut your eyes when you run? I warn you, sir, if you go shoving musketeers around, you'll be in for a thrashing."

"Then let us meet later," said d'Artagnan coolly.

"At one o'clock, then, behind the Luxembourg."

"Very well," said d'Artagnan.

Meanwhile the man with the scar had vanished. As d'Artagnan walked along he came upon Aramis chatting with three of the king's guards. He noticed that Aramis had just dropped his handkerchief and was now, no doubt unawares, standing on it.

D'Artagnan bent down, pulled the handkerchief from beneath Aramis's foot, and presented it to him. Aramis blushed scarlet and snatched it from his hands.

"Aha!" cried one of the guards, seeing the coat of arms embroidered on the handkerchief. "You cannot be on such poor terms with the gracious Madame de Bois-Tracy after all."

"You are mistaken, sir," Aramis replied, glaring at d'Artagnan. "It is not mine at all."

When the guards had gone, Aramis turned angrily on d'Artagnan.

"How could you be so stupid as to give me this handkerchief?"

"I saw you drop it."

"Let me repeat, this handkerchief never came from my pocket."

"Now you have lied twice, sir. I distinctly saw it fall."

"Oh, young Gascon. I see I shall have to teach you a lesson."

"Then draw your sword," said d'Artagnan.

"Not here. Meet me at Monsieur de Tréville's house at two o'clock," said Aramis.

The two men parted, and d'Artagnan set off for his first duel, with Athos at the Carmelite convent.

"I'll never get out of this alive," he muttered to himself. "Still, if I am killed, at least I shall be killed by a musketeer."

D'Artagnan pulled the handkerchief from beneath Aramis's foot.

Smooth operator
As King Louis XIII's chief minister, Cardinal Richelieu had immense political power in France. In 1623 he created his own group of guards, who were hated by the people and often clashed with the king's musketeers. The cardinal's guards wore red; the king's guards wore blue – a royal color.

Duelling © Disney
Richelieu had outlawed dueling by 1625, but it was still the favored way of settling arguments among hot-blooded gentlemen. Here Aramis (Charlie Sheen) duels with the cardinal's guards in Walt Disney's The Three Musketeers *(1992).*

D'Artagnan went swiftly to the deserted little piece of ground in front of the Carmelite convent. He arrived at this popular dueling place just as the clock struck the hour of noon. Athos was already there, waiting with Porthos and Aramis.

"What is he doing here?" asked Porthos, staring at d'Artagnan in astonishment.

"This is the gentleman I am to fight," said Athos.

"But I'm going to fight him," said Porthos.

"Not until one o'clock," said d'Artagnan.

"So am I," said Aramis.

"Not until two o'clock," said d'Artagnan.

Then he and Athos faced each other. Scarcely had they crossed swords when a squad of the cardinal's guards appeared, commanded by Monsieur Jussac.

"Aha!" cried Jussac. "You are well aware that dueling is against the law. Sheathe your swords, gentlemen; you are under arrest."

"That's quite impossible, sir," said Aramis, imitating Jussac's pompous tone.

"If you disobey the cardinal's order, we'll take you by force!" cried Jussac.

"There are five of them," Athos murmured to his comrades, "and only three of us."

"Gentlemen," d'Artagnan broke in, "it seems to me that there are four of us. I may not have the uniform, but I have the heart of a musketeer!"

Soon a terrific battle broke out. Athos took on Cahusac, one of the cardinal's finest swordsmen; Porthos fought grim-faced Bicarat, taunting and teasing him; and Aramis engaged the other two guards. D'Artagnan confronted Jussac himself. Though Jussac was an experienced soldier who relished a fight, he was soon bewildered by his opponent's speed. Losing his temper, he lunged wildly, and d'Artagnan, quick as a snake, thrust his sword into Jussac. The commander fell, and d'Artagnan sprang to help Athos, who had been wounded by Cahusac and now looked paler than ever. D'Artagnan soon sent Cahusac's sword spinning from his grasp, and Athos pierced him in the throat. Aramis, meanwhile, had killed one of his opponents and overpowered the other. Bicarat fought on, until Jussac, struggling to his feet, shouted at him to surrender.

The battle was over.

Soon a terrific battle broke out.

Word of the clash traveled quickly. That evening, King Louis, delighted that his men had come out on top, was in an excellent mood. He happily informed Monsieur de Tréville that the news of his guards' defeat had made the cardinal quite ill, and he asked to meet the musketeers and the young man who had done so well.

D'Artagnan and the musketeers celebrated with a fine meal.

Unfair to King Louis
Louis XIII had become king of France in 1610, when he was only nine years old. Although Dumas presents him as vain, secretive, and even cruel, he also was, in reality, a remarkably shrewd and skillful politician.

Chapter four

COURT INTRIGUES

WHEN THE MUSKETEERS and d'Artagnan were received by the king, he told them, with a twinkle in his eye, to stop feuding with the cardinal's guards. He also gave d'Artagnan a present of forty gold coins and ordered Monsieur de Tréville to find him a place in the Royal Guard.

Later d'Artagnan shared the money with the others and they celebrated with a fine meal. D'Artagnan did not have a valet, so Porthos presented him with a servant named Planchet. But the good times ended as the money ran out, and the four friends were soon so penniless and hungry that they were forced to scrounge meals.

One day there came a knock on d'Artagnan's door. On the threshold stood his landlord, a drab, rather shifty-looking little man named Monsieur Bonacieux. He told d'Artagnan that his young

wife, who was the queen's linen maid, had been kidnapped.

"Do you know who might have done this?" asked d'Artagnan.

"I'm not sure, but I suspect that it is part of a political intrigue."

"What on earth do you mean?"

"Four days ago my wife told me the queen was being persecuted by the cardinal and was very afraid. The queen believes that someone has been writing to the Duke of Buckingham in her name, in order to lure him to Paris and draw him into a trap."

"But the man who kidnapped your wife," d'Artagnan exclaimed, "what does he look like?"

"Dark, distinguished-looking, with piercing eyes and a scar on his cheek," said Bonacieux.

"A scar?" cried d'Artagnan. "It's the man from Meung!"

Monsieur Bonacieux pulled a scrap of paper from his pocket and handed it to d'Artagnan, "This came this morning."

> *"Don't try to find your wife or you are finished."*

"Will you help me, sir?" Bonacieux begged. "If you do, we'll forget about the rent you owe me. I will also offer you fifty gold pistoles ..." He suddenly broke off and pointed out of the window. "Who's that?"

A tall man, wrapped in a cloak, stood in a doorway on the opposite side of the street.

"That's him!" they cried with one voice. D'Artagnan drew his sword and ran out of the door.

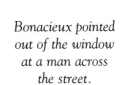

Bonacieux pointed out of the window at a man across the street.

Living it up
A musketeer was presumed to have private means – each was paid only 35 sous a day, a tiny amount of money. Athos, Porthos, and Aramis have a devil-may-care attitude to life, love, and money. They are nearly always broke and in debt, but they think nothing of spending the king's gift on a splendid meal.

Queen Anne
The daughter of King Philip III of Spain, Anne was only 14 when she married the young French king, Louis XIII. Her ties to Spain made the king and the cardinal suspicious of Anne throughout her life.

Royal favorite
George Villiers, Duke of Buckingham (1592–1628), was a favorite of the English royal family. His love affair with the French queen, Anne, is based on fact: on a state visit to Paris in 1625, he became infatuated with her.

D'Artagnan soon returned to his apartment to find the musketeers waiting for him. "That man must be the devil himself," he declared. "He disappeared like a ghost!" Then he told them about his plans to rescue Madame Bonacieux and help the queen.

"Why does the queen love those we hate most of all – the Spanish and the English?" mused Aramis.

"Spain is her home country," replied d'Artagnan. "It's quite natural. Besides, it's not the English she loves but an Englishman."

"Ah, yes," said Athos, "the Duke of Buckingham. A fine-looking man, I must admit."

"If we help them, it's also a defeat for our enemy the cardinal," said d'Artagnan. The musketeers swore their agreement, crying, "All for one and one for all!"

The next evening, a great tumult broke out in the apartment below d'Artagnan's. Listening through a hole in the floorboards, he heard a woman shout: "I tell you, I'm Madame Bonacieux, linen maid to the queen!"

Her cries were suddenly cut short.

"They're choking her, the cowards!" yelled d'Artagnan. "Quick, Planchet, my sword!" In an instant he jumped from the window down into the street and hammered on the front door. It opened and he charged inside, brandishing his sword. The lady's attackers ran for their lives.

"Hurry, Madame," he said, "those men were agents of the cardinal."

D'Artagnan led her to the safety of Athos's apartment. On the way she told him how she had earlier escaped her kidnappers by knotting her sheets together and climbing out of her prison window. She had then returned home and found four men waiting for her.

Mme. Bonacieux escaped her kidnappers by knotting her sheets together.

While she spoke, d'Artagnan was thinking how charming and pretty she was.

D'Artagnan drew his sword and challenged the man.

Bidding her a fond farewell, d'Artagnan went to Monsieur de Tréville and told him of the queen's predicament.

Some time later, d'Artagnan was wandering home through the streets of Paris, dazzled with love for pretty Madame Bonacieux. Suddenly, a woman escorted by a man dressed as a musketeer emerged from the darkness. Convinced that the woman was Madame Bonacieux, and gripped by jealousy, he challenged them. The two men drew their swords.

"Great heavens!" cried Madame Bonacieux, springing between them.

"You can't mean …" said d'Artagnan.

"Yes," said Madame Bonacieux in a low voice. "This is the Duke of Buckingham."

D'Artagnan stammered his apologies and escorted them to the Louvre, where the duke had a secret meeting with the queen.

The Louvre palace
Now a world-famous museum, the Louvre was then the main royal residence – a vast building with hundreds of rooms. Queen Anne had her own apartments, but finding privacy was difficult because of the network of spies.

Prison

Imprisonment without trial was common at this time. Prisoners were often tortured into confessing crimes they had not committed or left to languish for months without a chance to defend themselves. Bonacieux may be a coward, but his fears are well founded.

The cardinal's home

In 1624 Cardinal Richelieu started to build a residence near the Louvre. It was completed in 1636, and Richelieu later bequeathed it to the king. The building later became known as the Palais-Royal.

The spymaster

Cardinal Richelieu's power in the land is based on a complicated network of paid informers and spies. Dumas portrays him as a master manipulator.

M. Bonacieux quickly decided to tell the cardinal all he knew.

Chapter five

THE PLOT THICKENS

THE DAY AFTER his meeting with d'Artagnan, Monsieur Bonacieux was arrested and spent a sleepless night in a prison cell. The next day, he was dragged, shaking with terror, before Cardinal Richelieu himself.

Armand-Jean du Plessis, Cardinal Richelieu, was no more than thirty-seven at the time. He had a proud air and the look of a warrior, though his hair and beard were turning gray.

The cardinal spoke slowly. "You are accused of high treason. You have conspired with your wife and with the Duke of Buckingham."

Monsieur Bonacieux was not a brave man, and he quickly decided to tell all he knew. Under Richelieu's astute questioning he revealed the addresses of two

houses that his wife had recently visited. The cardinal rang a silver bell and sent for Rochefort.

A man with a scar on his cheek came into the room.

"That's him!" cried Bonacieux.

"What do you mean?" the cardinal demanded.

"The man who kidnapped my wife."

Richelieu ordered his guards to take this "imbecile" away. When they were alone, Rochefort informed him that the queen and the Duke of Buckingham had recently met in Paris.

"One of our agents, Madame de Lannoy, was there when the queen suddenly retired to her private chamber, accompanied by her maid. She was away for three quarters of an hour, and during that time the maid came back to fetch a small rosewood box."

"What was in the box?" asked the cardinal.

"Twelve diamond studs, your Eminence, a gift from the king."

"So the queen must have given the diamonds to the duke."

"I am sure of it."

The cardinal sent Rochefort to search the two houses visited by Madame Bonacieux. He also asked him to fetch her frightened husband again. This time he welcomed Bonacieux cordially. "You have done well, my good man," he said, giving him a purse full of money. "This will compensate you for being unjustly arrested. I hope that we shall meet again."

Bonacieux left the room babbling his thanks and crying, "Long live his Eminence!"

The cardinal then wrote a letter and gave it to his messenger.

"You will leave immediately for London," ordered Richelieu. "Take this letter and give it to Milady."

The letter said,

"Milady, go to the next ball attended by the Duke of Buckingham. He will be wearing twelve diamond studs on his doublet. Cut off two of them and report back to me."

A 17th-century purse

Purse
Richelieu is an expert reader of people. He quickly realizes that the cowardly, miserly Bonacieux will be easy to bribe. As the husband of one of the queen's most trusted servants, Bonacieux is likely to be a useful informer. Bonacieux is completely won over by the cardinal's power and money.

A French gold coin from the time of Louis XIII

Bonacieux left the room babbling his thanks.

A Spanish king
*In 1621, at age sixteen,
Philip IV became the king of
Spain. Like Louis XIII,
Philip was intelligent but
easily bored. He was greatly
influenced by his adviser,
Prime Minister Olivares, just
as Louis was by Richelieu.
Although Philip's sister Anne
had married Louis, relations
between the two countries
had not improved.*

Meanwhile Athos had been mistaken for d'Artagnan himself and arrested by the cardinal's men. When Monsieur de Tréville heard this, he went to complain to the king. At the palace, he came upon Cardinal Richelieu, who was furious about the young man who had put his men to flight and rescued Madame Bonacieux.

The king trusted the old commander of the musketeers, so de Tréville had little difficulty convincing him that Athos had been wrongly arrested. He also assured Louis that d'Artagnan had been dining with him at the time of Madame Bonacieux's rescue.

The cardinal bit his lip and bided his time. As soon as de Tréville left the room, he said,

"Sire, you should know that the Duke of Buckingham was in Paris for five days and left only this morning."

"By God," cried the king, turning pale, "do you think the queen has been deceiving me?"

Richelieu was delighted to see the king so upset.

"The queen may be conspiring against her king's power," he replied, "but surely not against his honor."

"Nonsense, cardinal," snapped the king peevishly. "I know the queen loves another. It must be that wretched Buckingham. She must have written to him. I want those letters."

"If you insist, Sire," said the cardinal. "I will have the keeper of the seals make a search."

Queen Anne flushed with anger when Séguier, keeper of the seals, announced his intention of searching her private rooms.

*"By God," cried the king,
"do you think the queen
has been deceiving me?"*

Before he could touch her, the queen pulled a letter from her dress.

When he searched and found nothing, Séguier declared that he would have to search the queen herself!

Before he could touch her, the queen pulled a letter from her dress and handed it to him.

"Take this, and free me from your odious presence," she said.

Séguier took the letter to the king, who saw that it was written to the queen's brother, the king of Spain. In it the queen asked him and the emperor of Austria, who strongly disliked Richelieu, to threaten France with war unless Cardinal Richelieu was sacked. King Louis, who had little interest in politics, was delighted that the letter made no mention of Buckingham or love. He showed it to Richelieu, who suggested that the king should make some amends to the queen for the indignity of having her rooms searched.

"May I suggest you hold a ball in her honor, Sire," he said smoothly. "She loves to dance, and it will give her a chance to wear those beautiful diamond studs you recently gave her."

Chapter six

THE QUEEN'S DIAMONDS

AS SOON AS the cardinal heard from Milady that she had two of Queen Anne's diamond studs in her possession, he fixed the date for the ball. It would be held at the Hotel de Ville in twelve days' time, on the third of October.

"And by the way, Sire," he reminded the king, "don't forget to tell her majesty how much you would like to see her wearing all twelve of the diamond studs you gave her." The king was baffled as to why Richelieu was so insistent about the studs. When he noticed the dramatic effect that any mention of the ball and the studs had on the queen, he was even more baffled. However, with such a cold and cruel nature, he enjoyed seeing her tremble under his gaze.

Louis enjoyed seeing Anne tremble under his gaze.

Diamond studs

A woman scorned
This episode was not invented by Dumas but based on a true account by the writer La Rochefoucauld. He relates that the diamonds were cut from Buckingham's doublet by a jealous lover, the Duchess of Carlisle.

"When is this ball to take place?" she asked him faintly.

"Very soon. I can't remember exactly; I'll have to ask the cardinal."

He departed, well pleased, leaving Anne in despair. She knew the ball was part of a plot to disgrace her, organized by the cardinal. The friendly voice of Madame Constance Bonacieux broke in on her dark thoughts:

"Let my husband go to London with a letter for Buckingham and recover the diamonds," she suggested.

The queen scribbled a note to the duke. Madame Bonacieux hurried home and told her husband to set out for London immediately.

"Oh, I see, another intrigue," he said grandly. "The cardinal has told me all about them."

He refused to go, praising Richelieu and patting the purse of silver the cardinal had given him. This infuriated his young wife.

"I knew you were a coward, a miser, and a fool," she shouted. "But to sell yourself to that devil for money!"

She quickly calmed down, realizing she had gone too far. Monsieur Bonacieux tried to worm out of her exactly why she wanted him to go to London, but his wife, now on her guard, pretended the matter was of no importance. Nevertheless, Monsieur Bonacieux decided to mention to the Comte de Rochefort that the queen was in need of a messenger. Claiming to have an appointment with a friend, he left the house.

As soon as she was alone, Madame Bonacieux heard a knock on the ceiling. D'Artagnan had overheard everything and was dying to prove his love for the pretty lady.

"Madame, let me offer my services and those of my friends, the musketeers."

Madame Bonacieux was hesitant, but when d'Artagnan assured her of his loyalty and love, she gratefully gave him the queen's note.

Suddenly they heard voices in the street – Monsieur Bonacieux was returning. They stole upstairs to d'Artagnan's apartment. From the window they glimpsed Madame Bonacieux's treacherous husband reporting to Richelieu's spymaster, de Rochefort, the man from Meung.

D'Artagnan wasted no time obtaining leave from Monsieur de Tréville for himself and the three musketeers to go to London.

The Hotel de Ville
This grand town hall, completed in 1628, was used for royal balls. Although it burned down in 1871, it was reconstructed some years later.

Postman's bag
A chain of messengers equipped with fresh horses was the fastest way of sending letters. Messages were carried in pouches like the one above, which belonged to a 17th-century military postman.

Mme. Bonacieux pretended the matter was of no importance.

Beauvais
The musketeers take the quickest route to Calais, stopping for the night in the main towns on the way. By the time he leaves Beauvais, d'Artagnan has already lost four of his companions, thanks to Richelieu's scheming.

The four adventurers and their servants left Paris at two o'clock in the morning. They traveled in silence, watching and listening for hidden enemies, until daylight broke. By eight they were in Chantilly, where they decided to stop at an inn. As they were eating breakfast, Porthos quarreled with a stranger who would not drink to the king's health. The others went on their way, leaving Porthos to fight a duel with the man.

Just beyond Beauvais they encountered a gang of men who seemed to be digging up the road. Aramis, annoyed by the prospect of dirtying his boots, swore at the men. The workmen snatched up hidden muskets from a ditch and opened fire. The travelers were riddled with shot, and Aramis was wounded in the shoulder.

The travelers were riddled with shot.

By the time they reached the next town, Aramis was in such pain that he asked to be left behind. Porthos had not appeared, so the others galloped on through the night.

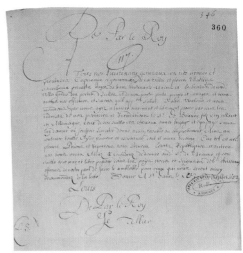

At Amiens, d'Artagnan and Athos took a room at an inn. Something about their host seemed odd, so the two servants stood guard through the night. When morning came, and Athos went to pay the bill, the innkeeper accused him of using counterfeit money.

"What a comedian!" cried Athos. "I'll cut your ears off!"

At that moment, four armed men ran in and set upon him. Shouting and firing two pistol shots, Athos just had time to warn d'Artagnan to flee. Of the eight men who had set off, now only d'Artagnan and Planchet, his servant, remained.

They rode on to Calais, only to find that the cardinal had issued an order that all travelers to England must have a special passport stamped by the governor of the port. Planchet pointed out a likely gentleman traveler and they followed him until they entered a wood on the way to the governor's house. D'Artagnan approached.

"Sir, I will be plain. I am on an urgent misssion and need the order that you have in your pocket," d'Artagnan explained.

"I presume you are joking, sir. I have to be in London by noon."

"And I have to be there by ten in the morning. I insist on having that pass," d'Artagnan repeated.

The man flatly refused and drew his sword. A vicious fight ensued, in which d'Artagnan wounded the stranger, leaving him unconscious. Searching the man's pockets, he found a pass in the name of the Comte de Wardes.

He presented the nobleman's papers at the governor's office.

"It seems the cardinal wants to prevent someone getting to England," the governor observed.

"Yes, a certain d'Artagnan; I know him well," said d'Artagnan, giving the governor a detailed description of the Comte de Wardes.

"We'll look out for him," said the governor, and stamped the pass.

An hour later, d'Artagnan was at sea, bound for England.

Passports
Even in the 17th century, identification was an essential part of traveling, especially overseas. D'Artagnan knows that he will reach England only if he uses someone else's passport – and in the days before photography and telecommunications, it was easy to take on a stranger's identity.

Faye Dunaway as Milady in
The Three Musketeers (1973)

Deadlier than the male
*Milady is the cardinal's top
agent. To men she makes
herself seem in need of
protection; to women she is
modest and sympathetic. One
by one, unsuspecting victims
are lured by her charms.*

Having a ball
*Balls were a highlight of
court life and allowed the
aristocracy to flaunt their
finery. To add extra interest,
balls often had a fancy-dress
theme. Guests were careful
not to upstage the king or
queen by wearing a more
splendid costume.*

Once on English soil, d'Artagnan immediately went to the Duke of Buckingham and gave him the queen's letter. The duke turned pale and led d'Artagnan straight to his mansion in London. There Buckingham unlocked the door to a very private room – a chapel lit by candles. Above the altar, below a canopy of blue velvet and ostrich plumes, hung a magnificent painting of the woman the duke worshipped: Anne of Austria, queen of France. Upon the altar lay the rosewood box containing the diamond studs she had given him.

He opened it – and uttered a terrible cry.

"What is it, my lord?" asked d'Artagnan.

"Two of the diamonds are missing! Stolen!" He thought for a minute. "This must be the work of the Countess de Winter, who stood close to me at a ball the other night. She must be the cardinal's agent."

Only five days remained before King Louis's ball. The duke called for his jeweler and ordered two replacement diamond studs, to be ready in two days. And to prevent the countess from reaching France, he stopped all ships leaving British ports.

As soon as the two new jewels were ready, the Duke made secure arrangements for d'Artagnan to sail to France. A relay of fresh horses then carried him onward, and in twelve hours he was safely back in Paris.

The king approached the queen, and saw she was wearing all twelve diamond studs.

The next day the Hotel de Ville was bustling with preparations for the ball. The king and queen arrived separately and went to change into their costumes. When the king was ready, handsomely arrayed in hunting dress, the cardinal showed him the two diamond studs that Milady had stolen.

"What does this mean?" asked the king.

"Nothing yet," said the cardinal mysteriously. "But if the queen appears wearing the diamonds, which I doubt she will do, count them, Sire. If she has ten instead of twelve, you might like to ask her how she lost the other two."

King Louis watched his wife enter, dressed as a huntress, and stared suspiciously at the cluster of diamonds she wore. The other guests sighed in admiration of her beauty, and the ball began.

When the dancing stopped, the king approached Queen Anne, and saw that she was wearing all twelve diamonds. She smiled sweetly as he turned his anger to the cardinal.

D'Artagnan, observing all this from the crowd, felt a light touch on his shoulder. He turned to see Madame Bonacieux, wearing a black velvet mask. She led him to the queen's chamber and told him to wait. After a while, a slender white hand appeared from behind a tapestry. D'Artagnan knelt and kissed the hand, which then withdrew, leaving a diamond ring in his palm.

Behind a mask
Sophisticated aristocrats of the time loved disguise and intrigue. At parties people often wore masks to help create an air of mystery and conceal their true identity.

St. Cloud
Today, St. Cloud is situated in west Paris, but at this time it was a separate village. Away from the many prying eyes of the city, St. Cloud was a good place to conduct a secret love affair.

Supper for two
Constance Bonacieux has prepared a special late-night supper for d'Artagnan. As shown in this 17th-century painting by Clara Peeters, such a meal might consist of wine, chicken, olives, a pastry, bread, and fruit.

Chapter seven

THE MEETING

D'ARTAGNAN HURRIED HOME to find a note from Madame Bonacieux. It said, *I want to thank you in my own way. Go to St. Cloud this evening at 10 o'clock and wait opposite the house of M. d'Estrées. C.B.*

He kissed the letter twenty times, then fell into a sleep of golden dreams. Later he called on Monsieur de Tréville.

"Be careful," warned the old commander. "The cardinal has a tenacious memory and a long arm. If I were you, I'd leave Paris immediately. Go to Picardy and find out what has happened to Athos, Porthos, and Aramis."

"I will leave tomorrow, sir, but this evening I have an essential appointment."

"Ah, young man, beware of women. They will be the end of us all."

On the stroke of 10 o'clock d'Artagnan was at the rendezvous in St. Cloud. Across the deserted street a solitary light burned in the first floor of a villa. Perhaps she is waiting for me there, he thought.

The half hour rang out from the St. Cloud belfry – a melancholy sound. There was still no sign of Madame Bonacieux.

D'Artagnan shivered, partly from cold, partly from a growing sense of unease.

By eleven he was really worried about her. He clapped his hands three times, the signal of lovers, but nothing, not even an echo, returned an answer.

The half hour rang out from the St. Cloud belfry.

There were clear signs of a violent struggle.

He climbed a tree and peered through the window of the villa. A supper table lay overturned and broken glass lay everywhere – clear signs of a violent struggle.

D'Artagnan jumped down. By the light from the window he noticed hoof marks and the tracks of a carriage. And there, lying in the mud, was a woman's torn, perfumed glove. He battered on the door of a nearby cottage. An old man appeared, and d'Artagnan begged him to tell what he had seen.

"Three men came to my door. They asked to borrow my ladder, and a short man with gray hair climbed up and looked through the window. Then he climbed back down and said, 'It's her.' Next thing, the men were inside the villa. There were terrible screams, and then they carried this woman out, threw her into the coach, and galloped away."

"What did their leader look like?"

"Tall, dark, with a scar on his cheek. Seemed like a gentleman."

"Him again!" cried d'Artagnan. "My demon!"

A 17th-century lady's glove

Kidnap clue
Before being carried off in the coach, Constance has cleverly left a clue that d'Artagnan will be likely to recognize – her glove.

"I'm dead drunk,"
Athos announced.

Wine cellar
Athos often seeks comfort in drink to drown his secret sorrows. His favorite drink is wine (especially from Anjou in the Loire district of western France), so what better place for him to hide than in the plentifully stocked wine cellar of an inn?

Chapter eight

THE HANGED WIFE

D'ARTAGNAN TOLD Monsieur de Tréville all that had happened to Constance Bonacieux. "I smell the work of the cardinal," said de Tréville. "You must leave Paris immediately. I will talk to the queen and see what can be done to help that poor woman."

Returning home, d'Artagnan encountered Monsieur Bonacieux outside the door of his house. The landlord's shoes were flecked with mud, just like his own.

A thought struck him. Could he have been the gray-haired man who went up the ladder last night? A husband who gloated over the kidnapping of his own wife? He felt like strangling the man. But first Porthos, Athos, and Aramis must be found. D'Artagnan hurried up to his apartment.

"Planchet!" he called. "Pack our bags. We leave in fifteen minutes." By retracing the route the musketeers had previously taken out of Paris, d'Artagnan soon found Porthos and Aramis. Both were resting up at inns, recovering from wounds. But what had happened to Athos?

At Amiens, the innkeeper told him that after d'Artagnan had ridden away, Athos had barricaded himself in the wine cellar and refused to come out. He had been in there ten days!

D'Artagnan took swift action and convinced Athos to open the doors.

"I'm dead drunk," Athos announced.

D'Artagnan calmed the innkeeper, then told Athos the news about Porthos and Aramis. He also related his own sad adventures with Madame Bonacieux.

"Ha! Love!" said Athos bitterly. "Love is a lottery. If you win, it kills you. Your story is a mere trifle. Want to hear a real love story?"

"Of course."

"One of my friends – a friend, mind, not I – was the lord of his province. At the age of twenty-five he fell for a beautiful girl of sixteen. Being an honorable man, he married her. The idiot!"

"But why, since he loved her?" said d'Artagnan.

"She was a perfect wife. One day they were out hunting and she fell from her horse and fainted. To prevent her from choking, the count cut open her riding habit. On her shoulder was a fleur-de-lys – the mark of a criminal condemned to hang. His angel was a devil who had somehow cheated the noose! To avenge the family honor, he took the law into his own hands. He hanged her on the spot."

"Good heavens! He murdered her!"

"Yes," said Athos, his face now deathly pale. "And that cured me forever of loving beautiful women."

Detail of a hunt on a 17th-century powder flask.

Hunting on horseback
Hunting was a popular pastime for the gentry, both men and women. Women often found it difficult to keep up because they had to ride sidesaddle; that looked elegant, but was unstable.

The fleur-de-lys
Criminals were often branded with a red-hot iron. There were different brands for different crimes. A fleur-de-lys marked the wearer for the ultimate penalty – death.

On her shoulder was a fleur-de-lys – the mark of a criminal condemned to hang.

The Church of Saint-Leu

Secret meetings
In those days of formal codes of behavior, church services provided ideal opportunities for men and women to make eye contact, meet, or make secret assignations. As d'Artagnan guesses, Porthos's reasons for going to church are not solely religious.

Chapter nine

MILADY AND A DUEL

D'ARTAGNAN was deeply shocked by Athos's story; he suspected that it was Athos himself who had taken the law into his own hands. But the next day, Athos laughed it off, saying he always told that story when he was drunk. They returned to Paris, picking up the others along the way.

Unfortunately, Monsieur de Tréville had no more news of Madame Bonacieux. The four friends also learned that they would have to join the siege of La Rochelle, and that they had just two weeks to equip themselves. It would cost two thousand livres each – a huge sum for a penniless musketeer. They looked at one another, flabbergasted. Then each went his own way, to see what money he could raise.

A few days later, d'Artagnan caught sight of Porthos going into the church of Saint-Leu. He followed him and hid behind a pillar.

The church was crowded, and during the sermon Porthos started making eyes at a beautiful woman sitting near the choir. This was clearly annoying another woman – older, with black hair – who was sitting near Porthos and flashing angry looks at him.

The woman near the choir made an impression on d'Artagnan, too. She was the woman he had seen in Meung, called "Milady."

After the service, d'Artagnan stood near her coach. He overheard her order the coachman to take her to the St. Germain district. Later that day, as he was riding along a quiet street in St. Germain, he came upon the same carriage, drawn up by the side of the road.

Milady was arguing in English with a richly dressed horseman. Suddenly she struck him with her fan, which broke into pieces. D'Artagnan saw his chance. "Madame," he said. "Allow me to punish this gentleman for his lack of courtesy."

"I would gladly agree," she replied, "but he happens to my brother."

"What does this idiot want?" asked the gentleman. At this, the two men started their own argument, and Milady drove away.

"Choose your longest sword and meet me behind the Luxembourg at six o'clock. My name is d'Artagnan."

"I am Lord de Winter. Do you have any friends who might also care for a fight?"

"I have three, sir," replied d'Artagnan.

St. Germain
On the left bank of the River Seine, St. Germain, then as now, was one of Paris's liveliest, most exciting districts. The musketeers would have known this part of town very well.

The fan
A fan was not just for keeping cool in a stuffy drawing room; it was an essential part of a lady's equipment. It could be used to conceal a whispered conversation, hide embarrassment, or convey a whole language of subtle signals. Folded up, it also makes a handy weapon, as Milady demonstrates.

Milady struck the gentleman with her fan.

At six o'clock, the four friends met their English opponents. Each exchanged names with his rival, as was the custom. Then the combat started.

The Frenchmen were in excellent form. With a brilliant flurry, d'Artagnan disarmed Lord de Winter and stood over him, his sword at the other's throat.

"I will spare your life, sir," he said. "Because I love the countess, your sister."

De Winter was delighted by d'Artagnan's chivalry and promised to introduce him to the countess that evening. D'Artagnan went home, changed into his finest clothes, and then called on Athos.

Athos shook his head gloomily, sensing that d'Artagnan was half in love with Milady already. "She's an agent of the cardinal," he warned, "and is sure to lead you into a trap. You've only just lost one woman, and now you're chasing another."

D'Artagnan disarmed Lord de Winter.

"Constance Bonacieux will always have my heart!" declared d'Artagnan. "But Milady greatly intrigues me. I want to find out all about her."

Shortly afterward Lord de Winter called to escort d'Artagnan to Milady's house in the Place Royale. There, in rooms furnished with remarkable splendor, she made d'Artagnan welcome.

"This gentleman held my life in his hands but let me live," said Lord de Winter. "Show him your goodwill, if you care for me."

A cloud seemed to pass over Milady's beautiful face, then she smiled. As de Winter described their duel in detail, d'Artagnan sensed her anger, though she did her best to conceal it. Lord de Winter, turning away to play with Milady's pet monkey, noticed nothing. Milady's maid, Kitty, then entered and spoke a few words to Lord de Winter. De Winter announced that urgent business called him away, and he left.

D'Artagnan was thus able to talk with Milady alone. He learned that de Winter was her brother-in-law, not her brother. She had married his younger brother, but he had died suddenly, leaving her

Milady's house
Milady's address in the Place Royale indicates that she is a woman of importance, for it was one of Paris's most select areas to live. The square of magnificent houses was built in 1609 and is now known as the Place des Vosges. During the 17th century, duels were often fought there.

D'Artagnan was captivated by Milady's charm and beauty.

a widow with a young son. The son was Lord de Winter's sole heir, if he died without marrying.

Captivated by her beauty, d'Artagnan visited Milady again the next day, and the next, and the next. Each time he left, he encounted Milady's pretty maid, Kitty. She gave him adoring looks, but his head was too full of thoughts of Milady to notice.

One evening Kitty was waiting for him when he arrived. "You may love my mistress, sir," she said boldly, "but she doesn't love you at all."

She showed him a note. "This is for the man she really loves – the Comte de Wardes."

At that moment, Milady called for Kitty. The maid went into the next room, leaving the door open. D'Artagnan could clearly hear their voices.

"I hate that Gascon," Milady was saying. "First he made me lose favor with the cardinal and then, instead of killing Lord de Winter, he spared his life. On behalf of my son, I would have inherited three hundred thousand francs. The cardinal has instructed me to handle him carefully," she continued, "but I'll get him one way or the other. Perhaps through Constance Bonacieux, that little mercer's wife he is so fond of."

In the other room, d'Artagnan shuddered and broke into a cold sweat. The woman was a monster.

41

Next day Milady was in a foul temper. She could not understand why the Comte de Wardes had not replied to her love letters. She never dreamed that d'Artagnan had snatched one from Kitty the night before. She wrote a stinging note to the count, but Kitty was so in love with d'Artagnan that she took that letter to him, too.

D'Artagnan wrote a reply in the name of the Comte de Wardes, promising that he would seek Milady's pardon at eleven that evening.

D'Artagnan had a reckless plan. He would go to the house, then slip into Kitty's room and surprise Milady by entering through the communicating door. He hated her, but he also felt a dangerous passion for her that he could barely control.

That evening she entertained d'Artagnan charmingly until ten o'clock. Then she began to fidget and cast anxious looks at the clock. D'Artagnan sensed she was growing nervous about her next appointment. He took his leave, then hurried up to Kitty's room. A few minutes later Milady called

D'Artagnan hurried up to Kitty's room.

She gave d'Artagnan a magnificent ring.

Kitty and ordered her to put out all the lights. She had decided to receive her lover, de Wardes, in darkness.

Shortly before eleven o'clock d'Artagnan entered her room.

Some hours later, as d'Artagnan took his leave, Milady said in her softest voice, "I am so happy that you love me, Count. I love you, too. Take this as a token of my feelings." And she gave d'Artagnan a magnificent ring, a sapphire surrounded by diamonds.

The next day, d'Artagnan told Athos of his adventure. When Athos examined the ring, he turned pale. "Give up this woman," he advised gloomily. "There is something fatal about her."

"You are right," said d'Artagnan. "She terrifies me."

He went home and found Kitty waiting for him. Her mistress was mad with love, she said, and wanted to know when he – or rather, the Comte de Wardes – would visit her again. D'Artagnan decided that this game had gone far enough. He took up his pen.

> Do not count on another meeting Madame. I am extremely busy at the moment. I will let you know when your turn comes round again.
>
> Comte de Wardes

"Impossible!" screamed Milady when the note was delivered. "No gentleman could write such a letter. I swear I'll have my revenge for this!"

A lady's boudoir
The boudoir was the most private room a lady had – an inner sanctum where she kept her most personal possessions, such as letters and love tokens.

Love letters
In the days before telephones and e-mail, letters were an essential way to conduct a love affair. Lovers often used coded language, where words were laden with hidden meanings. D'Artagnan's off-hand and blunt manner is deliberately insulting!

Goose-feather quill

A love letter

Fleur-de-lys

Branding iron

Marked for death

Milady is branded with a fleur-de-lys (the emblem of the French crown), a sign that she has been condemned to death. No wonder she wanted to keep the mark secret!

Chapter ten

THE FLEUR-DE-LYS

TO GAIN REVENGE on the Comte de Wardes for his insultingly heartless rejection of her, Milady turned to d'Artagnan. He soon felt himself falling ever deeper under the spell of her sparkling blue eyes and dazzling charm.

"I have a deadly enemy," she confessed.

"Just tell me what to do, Madame. I am ready to serve you."

"His name is ..."

"I know it already," cried d'Artagnan. "It is de Wardes."

"How do you know that?" Milady demanded.

"Yesterday I was at a salon and he was showing everyone a ring. He said that you had given it to him."

"The miserable dog!" cried Milady. Then she stopped. "Quiet. I hear my brother coming. You must go now. Come back and see me at eleven o'clock."

D'Artagnan left Milady's house. He returned as soon as the lights in her apartment were extinguished. As though in a dream he entered her private chamber. She used all her wiles to persuade him to murder de Wardes in a duel. "Are you afraid?" she asked.

"No," d'Artagnan blurted out, gripped by a sudden desire to deceive her no longer. "But I have something to tell you.

D'Artagnan saw at once the fleur-de-lys, the mark of the hangman.

The de Wardes you saw last night was not the real man. It was me."

She struck him and sprang away. D'Artagnan clutched at her robe. The fine material ripped, baring her shoulder, and to his horror d'Artagnan saw a strange burn mark on her white skin. It was a fleur-de-lys, the mark of the hangman. Milady was a condemned criminal!

She turned on him like a wounded panther. "You coward. Now that you know my secret, you must die!" She seized a dagger and leapt at him. D'Artagnan dashed into Kitty's room, bolting the door. Milady's dagger thudded into the wood; her furious screams rang through the house.

"Quick, put these on!" cried Kitty, throwing d'Artagnan a bonnet and an old dress. In this disguise, he stole out of the apartment and ran all the way to Athos's house.

"It's incredible," said d'Artagnan. "Milady has a fleur-de-lys branded on her shoulder!"

"Ah, no!" cried the musketeer, as if he had been shot.

"Listen," said d'Artagnan. "Are you sure the branded woman in your story who was hanged is really dead?"

In disguise, d'Artagnan stole out of the apartment.

Each quickly described the woman he knew. The descriptions matched exactly. Then Athos admitted that the sapphire ring Milady had given d'Artagnan was the very same one that Athos had long ago given to her.

"You are in mortal danger, my friend. Milady is the cardinal's most ruthless agent." He insisted on accompanying d'Artagnan to his house, where Kitty was waiting.

"I've run away from Milady," she said, trembling with fear.

Then Aramis arrived. He gave Kitty a letter to take to Madame Chevreuse, a lady who lived in the country. Once there, Kitty would be safe from Milady's anger.

D'Artagnan showed Athos the sapphire ring.

A cardinal's insignia on the front of a book.

Richelieu's books
Cardinal Richelieu was an avid book collector and built up a vast, impressive library in his palace in Paris. The library is not a typical place for a business meeting, but perhaps the cardinal wants to put d'Artagnan at ease.

Cardinal Red
Whereas blue was the royal color for the cloaks of the king's musketeers, the cardinal's guards wore red. Cardinals traditionally wore red to symbolize willingness to sacrifice their lives for their faith.

Chapter eleven

ASSASSINS

SEVERAL DAYS LATER, d'Artagnan received a letter telling him to present himself at the cardinal's palace at eight o'clock that evening. His friends, suspecting a trap, arranged to stand guard at the cardinal's gates for as long as d'Artagnan remained inside.

On his way there, a coach clattered by and a young woman stared out at him. D'Artagnan's heart leaped – it was Constance Bonacieux! She held a finger to her lips, warning him to remain still and not follow her.

"They must be taking her from one prison to another," thought d'Artagnan. "Will I ever see her again?" Sighing heavily, he walked on to the cardinal's palace.

A coach clattered by and a young woman stared out at d'Artagnan.

Cardinal Richelieu received him in his library.

"Now Monsieur d'Artagnan," he said, regarding the young man with piercing eyes. "I know exactly what you have been up to from the moment you came to Paris. It is my business to know everything. You are a brave man," he continued. "Even so, you have made some powerful enemies. Take care they do not destroy you."

"Alas, Monseigneur, they could do so very easily. They are strong and have powerful support. Unlike them, I am alone."

"That is true," said the cardinal. "But you have done a great deal on your own. However, I think you need some help. I assume you have come to Paris with the intention of making your fortune. So, how would you like to be an ensign in my guard?"

D'Artagnan looked embarrassed. "Oh, but Monseigeur, I am in the King's Guard."

"My guards also serve the king," the cardinal reminded him. "But speak your mind."

"It is only this," replied d'Artagnan. "The difficulty for me is that my friends are musketeers of the king, and by an awful coincidence my enemies happen to be in your guard. My friends would not be pleased if I accepted your offer. Perhaps," d'Artagnan went on quickly, "if I fight well at the siege, I will more fully deserve your gracious protection."

"My enemies are strong and have powerful support. I am alone," said d'Artagnan.

"So you refuse," said the cardinal. "Very well. I am not angry with you. But remember this. If something bad happens to you, it was I who tried to prevent it happening."

"Let what may happen, happen," said d'Artagnan, bowing as he withdrew. He felt a shiver of fear as he left the palace. The musketeers were waiting anxiously for him. A loud cheer greeted the news that d'Artagnan had refused a place in the cardinal's guards.

The next day, the four friends completed their preparations for war, and then went to a very noisy party together. At dawn they separated, and d'Artagnan rode away with the company of Monsieur des Essarts toward La Rochelle.

D'Artagnan was caught in an ambush.

Rebels in La Rochelle
The prosperous port of La Rochelle on the west coast of France had been a Protestant stronghold since the 16th century. In 1622 the town rebelled against the king, but after some resistance, tentative peace was established. At this point in the story (1627) another uprising has begun.

D'Artagnan's company pitched camp outside La Rochelle. Early one evening he was walking along a country lane, thinking about his problems. The last rays of the sun glinted on a piece of metal sticking through a hedge – the barrel of a gun. Then he noticed another on the other side of the lane. He was caught in an ambush. Two shots whistled past – he took to his heels. A third went through his hat. The hole was not made by a military weapon, and the cardinal had no need to set an ambush, he reasoned. This must be Milady's doing.

Two days later, two of the soldiers in d'Artagnan's reconnaissance party opened fire on him. A bullet killed one man and d'Artagnan fell across his body, pretending to be dead himself. The soldiers came nearer, intending to finish him off. Before they could reload their muskets, d'Artagnan sprang at them, his sword drawn.

He soon had the attackers at his mercy. One of them was carrying a letter. It said, *"Since you have lost track of that woman, and she is now in safety in the convent, take care not to miss the man; otherwise you shall pay dearly for the money I paid you."* There was no signature, but it was clearly from Milady.

"The queen must have found Constance and released her," d'Artagnan thought, "but where exactly is she being hidden now?"

A few days later d'Artagnan received twelve bottles of Anjou wine. An accompanying letter explained that the wine was a present from Athos, Porthos, and Aramis. D'Artagnan was delighted and organized a lunch party for two of his comrades. When the guests arrived, Planchet served the food and a new servant, Brisemont, poured the wine into carafes. He was then allowed to drink any dregs left in the bottles.

Before the guests could sample the wine, the king unexpectedly arrived in La Rochelle. His Majesty, escorted by Monsieur de Tréville's musketeers, had brought more troops to the battleground.

D'Artagnan went to invite Athos, Porthos, and Aramis to join his lunch party. "We can drink that wine you sent over," he added.

"What wine?" chorused the musketeers.

They rushed to the dining room. Brisemont was rolling on the floor having terrible convulsions. He had been poisoned by the wine and soon was dead. The four friends held a council of war. There seemed little doubt that the wine had been sent by Milady.

"I will expose that woman to the king if she does not cease these attacks on me," d'Artagnan vowed.

Constance was another matter. First of all, they had to find her.

"I will take on that task," said Aramis.

"You?" cried the others. "How will you do that?"

"Through the queen's chaplain," said the mysterious Aramis. "He and I are very close."

Weapons
Muskets used by the French army at this time were heavy and slow to reload. It was often more effective to use a sword in close combat, as d'Artagnan proves.

King Louis and the war
Despite falling seriously ill in July 1627 for over a month, King Louis had reached La Rochelle by October. Richelieu's personal control over the siege of La Rochelle had placed him in a position of great responsibility, and many people criticized him about the drawn-out nature of the war. When the siege eventually succeeded, Richelieu gained great respect from Louis for his political skill and insight.

Brisemont was rolling on the floor.

Inn
Inns were often used as secret meeting places, where amid the dark, smoky atmosphere, identities could easily be hidden. Innkeepers often kept private rooms for special guests.

Chapter twelve

THE RED DOVECOTE INN

ONE NIGHT Athos, Porthos, and Aramis were riding back to their camp from an inn called the Red Dovecote. On the road they encountered two horsemen. To their surprise, one of them was the cardinal himself, out on some secret mission. He ordered the three musketeers to escort him to the Red Dovecote.

"Monseigneur," said Athos, "there are some dreadful men in there. We had to give them a thrashing."

"What was your quarrel about?"

"A woman had just arrived at the inn. These wretched men were drunk and wanted to force open her door."

"Was she young and pretty?" inquired the cardinal.

"We didn't see her, Monseigneur."

Athos could hear voices coming from the room above.

Richelieu seemed pleased to hear that. They arrived at the inn, and he ordered the three musketeers to wait for him downstairs. Then the cardinal went upstairs alone.

Porthos and Aramis settled down to a game of dice, while Athos walked around the room, wondering about the identity of the mysterious person the cardinal had come to visit.

An old stove stood against the wall. Through its half-broken pipe, Athos heard voices coming from the room above.

"Milady," the cardinal was saying, "you are to sail tomorrow for England. Go to the Duke of Buckingham and tell him I will expose his affair with the queen if he makes one more move against France. Tell him I have all the proof I need."

"And if he refuses?"

"If he refuses, he will die."

"I shall see to it, my Lord," replied Milady. "And may I tell his Lordship about my own enemies? I need help to fight them."

"Who are your enemies?" asked Richelieu.

"Firstly, a meddling woman called Bonacieux. She is in a convent somewhere, and I am determined to find her. My other enemy is her lover, that miserable d'Artagnan."

"If you bring me proof that he has been dealing with the Duke of Buckingham, I will send him to the Bastille. From which he will not emerge."

"And now," Milady added quietly, "I require an order to grant me immunity for the actions I might need to take against our enemies."

"Give me a pen, ink, and paper," said the cardinal.

Athos had heard enough.

"If the cardinal asks for me," he said to the others, "tell him I've gone ahead to check our route home."

Then he slipped out into the night.

"My other enemy is that miserable d'Artagnan," said Milady.

The Bastille
The Bastille was originally built as a fortification to protect Paris against English attack. It was Cardinal Richelieu who first used it as a state prison. The Bastille soon became a symbol of terror: to be sent there was usually a death sentence.

Chapter thirteen

Heroes of Battle

La Rochelle
The siege of La Rochelle lasted 15 months. Richelieu's strategy was to build a sea wall across the harbor to keep out English ships bringing supplies to the town. This plan was so effective that by the time the Huguenot leaders surrendered, three-quarters of the town's population had starved to death.

ATHOS WAITED until the cardinal, his secretary, and the other musketeers left the inn. Then he crept up the stairs and silently entered Milady's room, pushing the door shut behind him.

Milady turned and shrank back as though she had seen a ghost.

"Who are you? What do you want?" she cried.

"Do you recognize me, Madame?" asked Athos, removing his hat.

"The Comte de la Fère!" gasped Milady.

She had spoken his name. It was all the proof he needed. Athos pointed a pistol at her head.

"Hand over that note the cardinal gave you, or I'll blow your brains out."

She obeyed, and Athos read the note:

"It is by my order and for the good of the State that the bearer of this note has done what he or she has done. Richelieu."

It was a note to pardon any action. Athos put it in his pocket, turned, and left the room.

Back at the camp the musketeers collected d'Artagnan and set off for another inn, where they could make plans without being overheard by the cardinal's spies. Unfortunately, the place was crowded with other soldiers who kept coming up to their table. So Athos made a daring bet with them. He and his friends would take their breakfast in an abandoned bastion under the noses of the enemy troops. To win the bet, they had to stay there for one hour, even if the enemy mounted an attack.

When they reached the bastion, they found it littered with dead bodies from an earlier fight.

"Leave them," ordered Athos. "They may be of use to us."

As the four friends settled down to talk, they saw an

enemy troop approaching. Immediately, they repelled them with sharp volleys from their muskets. Then Athos began to tell d'Artagnan about the cardinal's meeting with Milady. As he was showing him Richelieu's pardon note, the enemy surged forward again. This time the musketeers pushed over a wall, crushing most of the attackers.

The enemy regrouped and prepared to charge the bastion with an overwhelming force. Athos propped the dead bodies against the walls, putting muskets in their hands, so the invaders would think the bastion was strongly defended.

The musketeers resumed their talk. They decided to send one servant to warn Lord de Winter about his evil sister-in-law and another to Madame de Chevreuse so that she could inform the queen. By then the enemy were almost at the walls, and the four friends retreated to the camp. They had won their bet and were hailed as heroes.

That evening, d'Artagnan was received into Monsieur de Tréville's company of musketeers.

The musketeers pushed over a wall.

Chapter fourteen

DANGEROUS TIMES

THANKS TO THE WARNING sent by the musketeers, Milady was arrested as soon as she arrived in Portsmouth. Mad with rage, she was taken to Lord de Winter's castle and locked in a room.

"Do not let her out," Lord de Winter told her jailer, a stern naval lieutenant called Felton. Then he turned to Milady.

"This man is as cold as a piece of marble. You will get nothing from him. In two weeks' time you will be taken to rot in one of our most distant colonies."

At first, all alone, Milady despaired. Then she started to think. "I must use a woman's weapons and make my weakness my strength." A wild light of battle gleamed in her blue eyes.

When Felton entered the next morning, she pretended to be in a faint. His concern, although restrained, was obvious. So were his fanatical Puritan beliefs and thus his hatred of the Duke of Buckingham, whom he saw as an immoral Catholic sympathizer. Milady began to pray on her knees, ignoring the Catholic missal left at her feet and muttering about the plight of her "fellow Puritans." Felton felt ashamed about guarding such an innocent and beautiful creature. By the fourth day of Milady's imprisonment his sense of shame had grown; he was tortured by guilt and desire for his fair prisoner and begged her to confide in him.

She used all her wiles, spinning him a fantastic tale. The Duke of Buckingham, she claimed, had seduced and tortured her, and now Lord de Winter himself was in league with the evil duke.

"I want to die," she cried. "My shame is too great to bear."

"No, no," cried Felton, now completely under her spell. "You must live. You must have your revenge."

The next evening she heard tapping at the window. It was Felton. She climbed out and he carried her down a rope ladder. Quickly and silently they made their way to the beach. A sailing boat carried them out to another small boat. As they sailed toward Portsmouth,

*Felton carried Milady
down a rope ladder.*

Felton explained the next
part of his plan: "Lord de Winter is
sending me to see the Duke of Buckingham,
to have your deportation order signed. Tomorrow
the duke sails for France." There was a mad look in
his eyes. "But don't worry. He will not leave England."

The next day, claiming he had an urgent message from de Winter,
Felton was allowed to speak to Buckingham in person. Felton began by
protesting Milady's innocence, but when the duke refused to pardon her,
he drew a knife and stabbed him to death.

Milady was waiting on the shore. When she heard a cannon sounding the alarm, she
realized what Felton had done and immediately ordered the captain to sail to Boulogne.

Convent protection
Although nuns were not involved with worldly politics, the quiet confines of a convent were sometimes used to hide victims of persecution. But nowhere is entirely safe.

A nun's life
Discipline and simplicity were at the center of life in a Carmelite convent. Isolated from the outside world, the nuns spent much of their day in prayer and contemplation. Many nuns, like the abbess in this episode, came from aristocratic families, so they would have been familiar with court gossip.

Milady landed at Boulogne, in northern France. She sent word to Richelieu that the Duke of Buckingham had been either killed or gravely wounded. Then she set off, as previously instructed by the cardinal, for the Carmelite convent at Béthune, where she was to await further orders. Arriving there, she soon charmed the abbess with her talk of intrigues at court.

"We don't hear much about court life," said the Abbess. "But one of our novices has certainly suffered at the hands of the cardinal."

"I too have been a victim of the cardinal," said Milady, playing for sympathy, and asked to meet this poor novice. The abbess brought in a young woman. As they talked, Milady discovered that she was none other than the messenger to the queen and friend of the musketeers, Constance Bonacieux.

"Ah," cried Milady. "I don't know the musketeers myself, but my friend d'Artagnan knows them well."

"D'Artagnan!" Constance cried out in amazement. "Oh, you know him?" Then she added jealously, "What exactly is he to you?"

"Oh, nothing but a friend," Milady replied quickly.

"I love him so much, and he's coming here soon!"

"Here? But that's impossible ..." Milady froze as Constance produced a letter from Madame de Chevreuse confirming that d'Artagnan was on his way. Thinking quickly, she said, "Beware!

It's a trap. D'Artagnan and his friends are at La Rochelle. Servants of the cardinal, disguised as musketeers, are coming to take you away."

"How do you know that?"

"Believe me, dear Constance, I am all too aware of the cardinal's cruel nature. My sad life has been too full of these intrigues. We must hide somewhere in the neighborhood until my friends arrive."

Suddenly they heard the sound of horses galloping toward the convent. Milady ran to the window and recognized d'Artagnan at the head of eight horsemen.

"Quick!" she cried. "It's the cardinal's guards! We must go."

But Constance was too terrified to move. She fell to her knees. For Milady the day was lost, but she was still bent on revenge. She poured out a glass of red wine, emptied a small container of powder into it, and raised it to Constance's lips. The young woman drank. As though in a dream, she watched Milady dash from the room.

Constance felt weaker and weaker. Then there was banging at the door, and d'Artagnan and the musketeers burst into the room.

"D'Artagnan!" Constance gasped. "She said you'd never come."

"Who? Who?" demanded d'Artagnan.

"The countess," murmured Constance, and fell lifeless in his arms.

"My wife has done this," Athos announced to his astonished friends. "Leave her to me."

Poison could be easily disguised.

Hidden weapons
As a spy, Milady carries many secret weapons to use against the cardinal's enemies. But at this moment, Dumas implies that she is not driven by the cardinal's orders – she has become an evil force, who will stop at nothing to get revenge.

"D'Artagnan!"
Constance gasped.
"She said you'd never come."

Together they rode in silence through the darkness.

Athos smashed the window and vaulted into the room.

Chapter fifteen

DEATH SENTENCE

ATHOS GRIMLY set about forming his plans. He sent the musketeers' valets to search for Milady at all the inns along the roads between Béthune and Armentières. Then he visited a small, isolated house on the outskirts of Béthune.

A tall man opened the door, and Athos entered. He spoke briefly to the man and showed him a note, which had been signed and sealed. The man nodded his agreement, and Athos left.

Next day Planchet reported back. As Athos had suspected, Milady was staying at an inn in Armentières. But when the musketeers arrived there, a local man told them that she had left earlier that day and had taken a house somewhere near the river Lys. Athos sent a message to Lord de Winter, instructing him to join them.

It was a dark, stormy night. As the men saddled their horses,

a strange man joined them. He wore a mask and a large red cloak. Together the men rode in silence through the darkness toward the village of Erquinheim. As they approached, Athos's servant pointed to a little house by the riverside. A light shone from one of the windows.

Athos peered in and saw Milady seated before a dying fire. A horse whinnied, and she spun round. She saw Athos and screamed. Athos smashed the window and vaulted into the room as Milady ran to the door and flung it open. Standing there, pale as death, was d'Artagnan.

"What do you want?" cried Milady.

Athos came closer to her. "We have come to judge Anne de Breuil, also known as the Comtesse de la Fère and Lady de Winter."

First d'Artagnan, then Lord de Winter, and finally Athos accused Milady of a dreadful list of crimes, including the poisoning of Madame Bonacieux, complicity in the assassination of the Duke of Buckingham, and several attempts to murder Lord de Winter and d'Artagnan. Then the man in the red cloak stepped forward. He took off his mask and Milady gave a shriek of terror.

"It's the executioner of Lille!" she screamed. "Oh, forgive me!"

"Yes," said the man. "After you ruined the life of my brother, who later hanged himself, it was I who pursued and branded you with the mark you wear."

Athos asked everyone what sentence they demanded for Milady.

"Death," they all replied as Milady sank to her knees.

Lightning flashed as the execution party filed slowly down to the river. The executioner bound Milady's hands and feet.

"Cowards! Murderers!" she cried. "Ten of you against one woman!"

"You are not a woman," replied Athos coldly. "You are a demon escaped from hell. Now we are sending you back there."

Milady began to scream, and suddenly d'Artagnan could bear it no longer. "I can't watch her die like this," he moaned, moving toward her. At once Athos drew his sword to prevent him. "Headsman, do your duty!" he called. The executioner placed Milady on a boat, which slid across to the other side of the river. As the men fell to their knees and prayed, they saw Milady crouched on the far bank. The executioner's sword rose, moonlight glinting on its blade. Then it flashed downward.

River Lys
The river Lys runs across the border of Belgium and France, by Armentières. Lys means lily – a flower that symbolizes purity. Dumas's setting for this episode is deliberately ironic: the evil Milady is comdemned to die on the banks of the river of purity.

The boat slid across to the other side of the river.

D'Artagnan's statue is in
Auch, in Gascony.

Gascon hero

*The real d'Artagnan, whose
name was Charles de Batz-
Castelmore (he inherited the
title of M. d'Artagnan from
his mother) did not become
a musketeer until 1644,
when he was 29. By the
time he was made captain-
lieutenant, d'Artagnan was
52, not in his twenties as
Dumas suggests.*

Christopher Lee as the
man from Meung.

Mystery man

*Dumas's mysterious man, de
Rochefort, is a largely
fictional character, although
the name appears in
Courtilz's* Mémoires de
Monsieur le Comte de
Rochefort *(1678).*

Chapter sixteen

THE FOURTH MUSKETEER

THE FOUR FRIENDS felt a great sense of loss and melancholy. One evening they were sitting silently in a café when a familiar figure appeared.

D'Artagnan shouted for joy. It was his phantom, the man from Meung. He drew his sword, but the man addressed him politely.

"This time it is I who am looking for you," he said. "My name is de Rochefort, and I arrest you in the King's name. I have orders to bring you before Cardinal Richelieu."

The musketeers would have sprung to d'Artagnan's aid, but he saw little point in resistance. On the condition that his friends could act as his escort, he surrendered his sword to de Rochefort, and the party set off for the town of Surgères, where the cardinal was residing.

The next day, d'Artagnan was taken before the cardinal.

"Do you know why you have been arrested?" Richelieu asked.

"No, your Eminence. But I imagine it must be the work of a certain woman – a woman who was branded a criminal, who poisoned her second husband, and who tried to poison me too."

"Who are you talking about?" asked the cardinal.

"Milady de Winter. And now she is dead, Monseigneur."

"Dead?"

Then d'Artagnan told the cardinal how they had judged and executed Milady. The cardinal shivered.

"You will stand trial for this," he said.

"I am ready for that, Monseigneur," said d'Artagnan. "But you have already pardoned me."

"I have? Are you mad?" cried the cardinal.

D'Artagnan pulled out a note. Richelieu recognized it as the one he had given Milady at the Red Dovecote, giving the bearer a free hand to act as he or she pleased in the name of the state. Now d'Artagnan was the bearer.

The cardinal stared at d'Artagnan's honest, intelligent face, noting the tears of grief running down his cheeks. A man of such courage

D'Artagnan fell at the Cardinal's feet.

and loyalty could do great service. He tore up the note and went to his desk.

"I am doomed," thought d'Artagnan, as Cardinal Richelieu began to write on a piece of parchment.

The cardinal handed it to him. "Put your name here," he said.

D'Artagnan looked down fearfully. Instead of a death sentence, it was a lieutenant's commission in the musketeers! He fell at the cardinal's feet.

"Monseigneur, I am not worthy of this. My three friends deserve it much more ..."

"Take it and do what you please with it," said the cardinal. He called for de Rochefort. "From today, Monsieur d'Artagnan is my friend," he announced. "You two must embrace and be more careful in future."

The two enemies embraced, without much enthusiasm, knowing that they would meet again someday.

D'Artagnan returned to his friends and tried to persuade them that they were more deserving of the commission than he, but they waved his protestations away. To settle matters, Athos wrote d'Artagnan's name on the parchment and placed it in his hand.

"You deserve this more than any of us," he said. "Today you may have bitter memories. But you are young. In time bitterness will turn to happiness. Believe me."

Dumas's heritage

Dumas came from an unusal family. His father was the illegitimate son of an aristocrat, Antoine Alexandre Davy (who had moved to the Caribbean in the late 18th century), and a former slave girl. Dumas's father became a soldier, and soon rose to the position of general in the revolutionary and Napoleonic armies. But his outspoken manner led to his downfall. When he disagreed with Napoleon's strategy, he was forced to retire. He died four years later, leaving his wife and young son, Alexandre, penniless.

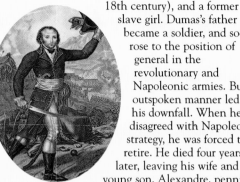

The early years

Alexandre was brought up by his mother in the small town of Villiers-Cotterêts. Though he had little formal education, spending much of his childhood playing in the nearby forests, his flamboyant personality gave him a love of drama. When a group of traveling actors passed by, he discovered Shakespeare, and decided he would be a dramatic author. By the age of 21, his beautiful handwriting helped him to find work as a clerk in Paris.

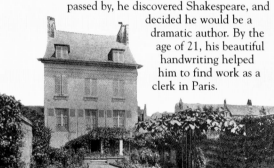

Popularity

Dumas's boundless energy and original ideas earned him friends and admirers in the theater, and success on the stage. He was soon involved in the Romantic literary movement, changing the face of theater and attracting huge audiences, who were captivated by his powerful productions. He became a very popular figure, especially with women, who loved his charm and his skill as a dancer.

History comes alive!

In 1841 Dumas discovered some memoires about musketeers in Louis XIV's time, written by Courtilz. By rewriting these stories, Dumas transformed these historical characters into romantic heroes. When his swashbuckling suspense story was published as a serialized novel called *The Three Musketeers*, Dumas's popularity soared. Over the next few years, he wrote a vast quantity of historical novels, including the bestseller *The Count of Monte Cristo*.

DUMAS'S WORLD

Despite being a general's son, Alexandre Dumas (1802–70) was brought up in poverty. As a young man, he traveled to Paris and set about educating himself by reading novels and going to the theater. He soon discovered a talent for writing and embarked upon a hugely successful career, first as a creator of exciting plays and later, of bestselling historical novels. He was generous, enthusiastic, and adventurous; his life was almost as exciting as the stories he told.

Victor Hugo's "Salon": Gautier and Dumas (standing).

Romantic times

By the time Dumas was in his twenties, a new spirit dominated the literary and political world. It became known as Romanticism. The Romantics championed a life of "passion" and "freedom" over "reason." This spirit was, in France, a movement of the young against the old, of the individualist against the establishment. As the grandson of a black slave and the dashing son of a revolutionary general, Dumas never lost touch with this movement. He became friends with the writers Victor Hugo, Charles Nodier, and Théophile Gautier (shown above) and remained passionately in favor of the individual and liberty for all.

Adventures abroad

One of Dumas's great passions was travel. In Russia and North Africa, as well as large areas of Europe, Dumas was excited by the new ideas and cultures he experienced. On a visit to Italy, he encountered the soldier Garibaldi (who helped unify Italy several years later). Dumas became involved in Garibaldi's struggle, sending him money and support for his cause.

Dumas edited an autobiography of Garibaldi, the Italian soldier and patriot who fought for the unification of Italy.

Home Comforts

Dumas's imagination did not stop with his fiction. The great success of his novel *The Count of Monte Cristo* enabled him to build his dream home – an extraordinary house surrounded by moats, with a Gothic pavilion set in the middle of an English-style park. Dumas named it "The Château de Monte-Cristo." Dumas's extravagance meant his money did not last long, and he had to write prolifically to make ends meet, working through the night to get projects finished on time. Despite his efforts, by the end of his life he was still in debt and, like his father, died penniless.

Dumas's Château de Monte-Cristo

LONG LIVE THE MUSKETEERS!

The fame of d'Artagnan and the three musketeers did not end with the passing of the 19th century. Just as Dumas's characters and plots were relished during his life, so the 20th century found endless excitement in retelling his stories on film and television. Even today, Dumas is one of the best-known and most translated French novelists.

Michael York, Frank Finlay, Oliver Reed, and Richard Chamberlain take up their muskets again.

Timeless dueling in The Count of Monte Cristo *(1934).*

All for one and one for all!

In *The Return of the Musketeers*, (1989) the stars of Richard Lester's earlier film *The Three Musketeers, The Queen's Diamonds* (1973) returned to play the four friends again (shown above).

Hound dog!

In the world of cartoons, d'Artagnan became *Dogtanian* – a dog who helps his three muske*hounds* defeat a scheming cat, Milady!

History repeating

Whether the stories are retold to fit the age they are made for (as above) or set as a period drama, characters such as the Count of Monte Cristo, Milady, and Richelieu remain as vivid as they were to Dumas' first readers. The combination of suspense, romance, and action is timeless!

Leonardo DiCaprio in The Man in the Iron Mask *(1997).*

Acknowledgements

Picture Credits
The publisher would like to thank the following for their kind permission to reproduce the photographs.

t=top, **b**=bottom, **a**=above, **c**=center, **l**=left, **r**=right.

Archive Photos/The Image Bank: 8tl;
Bibliothèque Nationale, Paris: 16tl; 26tl; 50t;
Bridgeman Art Library: 8bc (Gerrit van Honthorst, "George Villiers, First Duke of Buckingham"; Philip Mould, Historical Portraits Ltd., London); 8bcr (Philippe de Champaigne, "Louis XIII Crowned by Victory"; Louvre, Paris/Giraudon); 18tl (Philippe de Champaigne, "Cardinal Richelieu"; Château de Versailles); 22t (Peter Paul Rubens, "George Villiers, 1st Duke of Buckingham"; Palazzo Pitti, Florence); Velasquez, "Philip IV on Horseback"; Prado, Madris;
British Film Institute: 60b;
Photographie Bulloz: 8tcl; 10tr; 24cl; 51b;
J. Allan Cash: 13tr;
Jean-Loup Charmet: 8tcr; 11tr; cr; br; 23b; 29b; 31t; 32b; 37t; 46t; 62tl; tr; cl; 63tl; tr;
Château de Saumur: 44tl;
Christie's Images: 25cr;
Corbis: 30t (Seattle Art Museum); 36b (Dave Bartruff);
Samuel Dhote: 59t;
ET Archive/Prado, Madrid: 34t;
Mary Evans' Picture Library: 11bl; 15tr;
Eye Ubiquitous/Mike Southern: 54t;

Ronald Grant Archive: 11tl; cl; 32t; 46bl; 63cr;
Jacquie Gulliver: 40b;
Hulton Getty: 8bl; 21br;
Kobal Collection/© Disney: 18cl;
The Moviestore Collection: 10tl; 63cl; bl; br;
© **Photo Musée de l'Armée, Paris:** 10bl; bcl; bcr; br; © **Musées de la Ville de Paris:** 20bl (D. Lifermann); 25tr; (P.Ladet); 29t; 49cr;
From the collection of the Worshipful Company of Glovers of London on loan to the Museum of Costume, Bath: 35b; by courtesy of the **National Portrait Gallery, London:** 54c;
© **Photo RMN:** 52t (Versailles & Trianon);
V & A Picture Library, London: 39b;
Roger-Viollet: 13br; 21tr; 56tl; 62cr;
Reproduced by permission of the Trustees of the **Wallace Collection, London:** 43tr;
Warwick Castle: 49t;
Wilberforce House Museum, Kingston upon Hull: 44tl

Jacket:
Jean-Loup Charmet: Back flap tl.
Château de Saumur: Front cover c; Back cover c.
Christie's Images: Front cover tl.

Photography: Andy Crawford at the DK Studio.

Additional Illustration: Sallie Alane Reason, John Woodcock.

Calligraphy: Stephen Raw.

DK Publishing would particularly like to thank the following people:

Mark Regardsoe for design assistance; A.K. Wallersteiner for his help on historical background; Prof. C. Thompson for his advice as consultant; Jill Bunyan for DTP assistance; Catherine Costello for additional picture research; Rebecca Smith for hand model.